Dolores

by *Barbara Samuels*

Ink

Dorling Kindersley Publishing, Inc.

A Melanie Kroupa Book

Dorling Kindersley Publishing, Inc.
95 Madison Avenue
New York, New York 10016

Visit us on the World Wide Web at http://www.dk.com

Dorling Kindersley books are available at special discounts for bulk purchases for
sales promotions or premiums. Special editions, including personalized covers, excerpts
of existing guides, and corporate imprints can be created in large quantities for specific needs.
For more information, contact Special Markets Dept.,
Dorling Kindersley Publishing, Inc., 95 Madison Ave., New York, NY 10016; fax: (800) 600-9098.

Library of Congress Cataloging-in-Publication Data

Samuels, Barbara.
Aloha, Dolores / by Barbara Samuels. —1st ed.
p.   cm.
"A Melanie Kroupa book"
Summary: Certain that they will win a trip to Hawaii, Dolores enters her cat,
Duncan, in the Meow Munchies contest and goes all out preparing for their trip.
ISBN 0-7894-2508-4
[1.Contests—Fiction. 2. Cats—Fiction. 3. Hawaii—Fiction.]
I. Title.
PZ7.S1925A1   2000
[E]—dc21   97-52104 CIP AC

Book design by Chris Hammill Paul. The illustrations for this book were painted with watercolor.
The text of this book is set in 15 point Calisto.

Printed and bound in U.S.A.
First Edition, 2000

2   4   6   8   10   9   7   5   3   1

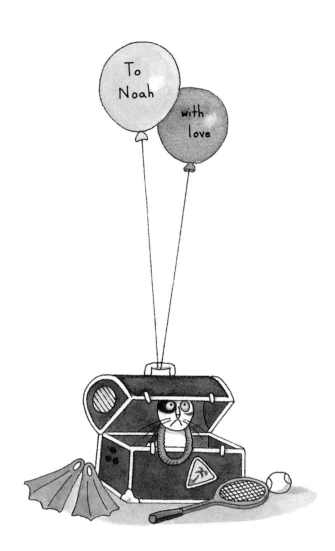

It all began one morning
when Faye and Dolores were
buying cat food for Duncan.

"What's this?" asked Dolores.

Faye picked up a box of Meow Munchies
and read aloud from the back.

"Wow!" said Dolores.

"Duncan won't even *eat* Meow Munchies," said Faye.

"He doesn't have to," said Dolores. "Pretty soon we'll both be eating pineapples and coconuts."

"So why *does* Duncan deserve the best?"
Faye asked when they were almost home.

"That's easy," said Dolores. "Because he's
good-looking, smart, and loaded with talent."

"Talent?" said Faye. "Duncan?"

"He's very good at hiding, and he can play the guitar," said Dolores.

"You can't count the time you dropped a tuna sandwich on the strings and Duncan licked them," said Faye.

"Why not?" said Dolores. "Write that down for me, Faye."

"Now smile, Duncan!" said Dolores when she got home.

She took one picture . . .

and another . . .

and another . . .

"You can't send one of *those*!" said Faye.

"I know," said Dolores. "He looks so handsome it's hard to choose just one. I'll send them all."

Dolores spent the afternoon
shopping for her trip.

The next day at Show and Tell
she announced that Duncan was
going to win the Meow Munchies
contest. Then she did a short
hula demonstration.

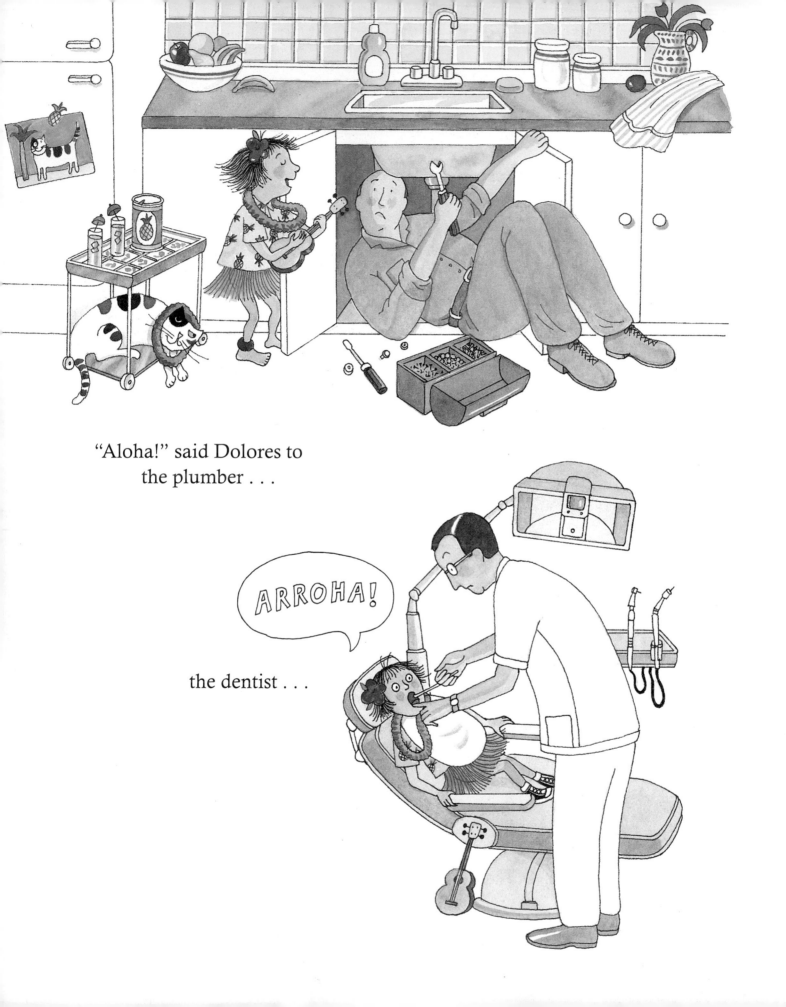

"Aloha!" said Dolores to
the plumber . . .

the dentist . . .

and the people
on the crosstown bus.

Before long the whole neighborhood knew that Dolores would be leaving for Hawaii soon.

"Listen," said Faye one day.
"Hundreds and thousands of
people want to win the
Meow Munchies contest."

"That's why it will be so great when they pick me!" said Dolores.

The day the winner
was to be announced,
Dolores packed her bags.

That night Faye was listening to the radio when an ad for Meow Munchies came on.

CONGRATULATIONS to Fifi, a Siamese from Southpaw, Indiana, our new Meow Munchies winner! "Fifi is a princess, she inspects her dish each day. If it isn't Meow Munchies she sniffs and walks away!"

"I can't believe a cat named Fifi
won the contest!" cried Dolores.

"Are you okay, Dolores?"
Faye asked a little later.

There was no answer, just
the sound of sniffling and
the plinking of a ukelele.

Faye disappeared. Soon she was back with a tray.
"Aloha, Dolores!" she said.

"How could they choose Fifi?" cried Dolores.
"Duncan is so upset! Now we'll never get a chance
  to hula and snorkel and have a luau!"

"But you already did all those things," said Faye.

Dolores thought for a moment. She held up an empty scrapbook.

"I was going to fill this up with pictures of my trip."

The two sisters looked at each other.

"Well?" said Faye.

"I'll get the camera," said Dolores.

"I'll get the pineapple juice," said Faye.

BON VOYAGE!

MY SHIP

CATCHING SOME RAYS

HULA NIGHTS

The next day Dolores brought her
Hawaiian scrapbook to Show and Tell.
Everyone agreed it must have been
quite a trip.

That night Faye noticed
that Dolores had put away
her grass skirt.

"I guess you don't care about Hawaii
  anymore," she said.

  Dolores smiled mysteriously.
"Duncan and I have made other plans."

"Olé!"